AF173937

Dead Accounts

Theresa Rebeck

A SAMUEL FRENCH ACTING EDITION

SAMUEL
FRENCH
FOUNDED 1830

SAMUELFRENCH.COM
SAMUELFRENCH-LONDON.CO.UK

FOR PRODUCTION ENQUIRIES

UNITED STATES AND CANADA
Info@SamuelFrench.com
1-866-598-8449

UNITED KINGDOM AND EUROPE
Plays@SamuelFrench-London.co.uk
020-7255-4302

Each title is subject to availability from Samuel French, depending upon
country of performance. Please be aware that DEAD ACCOUNTS may
not be licensed by Samuel French in your territory. Professional and
amateur producers should contact the nearest Samuel French office or
licensing partner to verify availability.

MUSIC USE NOTE

IMPORTANT BILLING AND CREDIT REQUIREMENTS

DEAD ACCOUNTS was first produced by The Shubert Organization at the Music Box Theatre in New York City. The opening date was November 29, 2012. The performance was directed by Jack O'Brien, with sets by David Rockwell, costumes by Catherine Zuber, lighting by David Weiner, and composition/sound design by Mark Bennett. The Production Stage Manager was Rolt Smith. The cast was as follows:

JACK . . . . Norbert Leo Butz

LORNA . . . . Katie Holmes

JENNY . . . . Judy Greer

PHIL . . . . Josh Hamilton

BARBARA . . . . Jayne Houdyshell

CHARACTERS

JACK

LORNA

JENNY

PHIL

BARBARA

SETTING

Cincinatti, Ohio

TIME

Present

FROM THE PLAYWRIGHT

America doesn't know how to talk to itself anymore.

It wasn't always like this. I was born and raised in the Midwest, where people were taught that decency and integrity and community were all important values. We were Democrats with a little 'd.' We were told that hard work and talent and character would get you somewhere. At school, we learned it was important to share. On Arbor Day, we all planted trees.

And we admired the people who lived and worked on the East Coast. Writers like Arthur Miller and Tennessee Williams were heroic figures. The great museums and orchestras and universities were, to us, the jewels of American accomplishment. It was an unimaginable thrill, to go New York and see the Statue of Liberty and the Empire State Building and Times Square. To see a play on Broadway – which cost I think about twenty-five dollars – was a dream beyond dreaming.

I don't know what New Yorkers thought about Midwesterners during those years – and this wasn't all that long ago; I'm actually not a hundred years old. I do know what New Yorkers think of the Midwest now, and I know what the Midwest thinks of New York. When I go to Ohio to visit relatives on holidays, I am often astonished by the level of casual dismissal which is offered up by way of discussion. At a time when the country faces deeply complex challenges around its future and the future of the planet itself, there is a sense that only crazy East Coast liberals worry about that stuff.

There is a sense that the East Coast has lost its moral center. The catastrophe of the banking industry, and the scandalous waste of our character, perpetrated by our government and the media has offended the Midwest so deeply they don't want to even talk about it. Or, they do want to talk about it, but they are so angry and simultaneously so polite, they don't know how to talk about it. So they bury their heads in Fox News and pretend that reducing the deficit will salve their anxiety.

Meanwhile, the East Coast cannot believe how stupid the center of the country seems to have gotten.

How do you make this funny? There are times when I wonder how I ever thought that I could dramatize the death of a national discussion as a family comedy. But so many of us are the spawn of this perplexing divide; we carry it in our DNA. The question – How did we start there, and get here? – is in fact a question of mortality. Which, as we all know, is hilarious.

Death is coming to our little family, and so we fight to live. Peculiarly, that is funny. And we do have things to teach each other. As long as we can remember how to talk.

– *Theresa Rebeck*

THE LIFE IN *DEAD ACCOUNTS*

In a life and career that has embraced nearly as many styles and opportunities as there are theatrical genres, Rebeck's DEAD ACCOUNTS was my first encounter with her world and her magic; and I trust and pray, not my last!

On the surface, of course, this is a wry, witty, caustic tale of a young man going to ground in his parents' home in Ohio having somehow siphoned off twenty-seven million dollars from a New York bank without anyone knowing about it. But the surface only glitters and enchantingly distracts in Ms. Rebeck's world from deeper shadows and shuddering shoals below. People are never quite how they represent themselves, and the baffling game of life is a canvas upon which she can splay, flay, and dissect her characters with the skill and precision of a surgeon, and the romantic tough of a jazz pianist.

Music is very much a part of this experience, as a swift reading of any of the major passages will reveal: she stutters, she stammers, she articulately skips from subject transition like a dizzy aerialist at the top of a tent, and my first direction to the company was to meticulously care for and replicate each and every ellipse, each unfinished thought until her cadence was second nature to them. But stretching still beyond for us was the play's mystery... what was pulling Jack on, what was compelling him, and what was drawing all the other relatives and characters in his boiling wake? Daily, we searched, asked, and questioned the text for its secrets.

And one other thing: at the end of the play, Ms Rebeck calls for a kind of coup de theatre – a dissolving of the entire set to reveal a glorious Midwestern autumn vista and a tree, planted by Jack himself, that seems to be the final message. She offers no clues, she never explains herself, she seems to trust in the ineffable mystery of life, a life she renders with exquisite care and infinite patience, believing that we, too, will fall under the spell of her characters as she has, and therein, ferret out our own explanation. Because life itself offers no explanations, and the great writers, Shakespeare, Corneille, Shaw, de Vega, as well as the classic modernist, most especially the "good Doctor" Chekhov, whose tragicomic world she so completely understands, never tell us what to think, they allow us our own conclusions. And we are always grateful to be led, rather than instructed.

A wise director makes no assumptions, and no predictions. He directs, he doesn't qualify but this modern fable or morals, money, and mystic magic, I sense will be tempting us for years to come. What a breathtaking ride!

– Jack O'Brien
New York City
November 3, 2012

ACT ONE

Scene One

(*A suburban American kitchen in Cincinnati, Ohio.*)

(**LORNA** *watches* **JACK** *eat ice cream from the carton. The kitchen table is covered in cartons of Graeter's ice cream.*)

JACK. This stuff is awesome. Does it still have the giant chunks in it? Like if you get lucky you can find just a, I love that, those giant chunks of, this stuff is amazing.

(*He attacks the ice cream carton.*)

LORNA. Do you want a bowl?

JACK. No, this is fine. This is awesome. This is like, you know, it's like the best ice cream in the world. People in New York go 'oh there's this great place in Brooklyn' or 'there's this gelato place on the Upper West Side' and I'm like you people have no idea. The best ice cream on the planet is in Cincinnati, Ohio. And they are so fucking superior! 'Cincinnati? Really?' Like that's the most, it's just retarded, honestly. So fucking retarded! You know you can get them to ship it. You can have them put a whole shitload of ice cream in dry ice and have it shipped for like, you know, not that much money when you think about it, and I was going to do that? Just to prove a point? But then I thought, no fuck you all. I don't have to prove anything. You all can just go to your graves without tasting Cincinnati ice cream. You don't deserve it! You just don't deserve it.

(*He continues to eat.*)

LORNA. Mom didn't tell me you were coming.

JACK. No, I wanted to surprise her. Well, I surprised myself, too. I mean, I didn't, she didn't know, and I didn't know either, until I got on the fucking plane.

LORNA. You…

JACK. That's what happened! It is! I just, walked out of my building and thought FUCK THIS BULLSHIT I'M GOING TO FUCKING CINCINNATI, and then, next thing I knew I was on a fucking airplane. Which is, why not, why the fuck not. That fucking city. You were right, that place is fucked up.

LORNA. Hey, Jack, you know I don't want to, but Dad especially is still a little sensitive about the language thing and if he wakes up –

JACK. I thought he was all fucked up on Percoset.

LORNA. He's in a lot of pain so yeah he is on something but

JACK. How high's the dosage? Because Percoset is fine but if he's in like a LOT of pain they should be giving him oxycotin. That stuff will really fuck you up.

LORNA. I don't know what he's on.

JACK. That stuff will make you puke, that's how strong it is, it's like heroin, unbelievable, if they're not going to give out morphine – did they give him morphine?

LORNA. I don't –

JACK. If he's in a lot of pain they should have him on something good.

(He opens another carton of ice cream.)

This stuff is unbelievable. I got off the plane, I'm like I have got to get some fucking ice cream; this is no joke. I'm hungry, like so fucking hungry, it's like primal hunger, I could eat a fucking wild boar, raw, but you know what time it is?

LORNA. Well, it's after twelve now –

JACK. Right? Right? So I'm in the parking lot of Graeter's, the one on Kenwood Road? And the place is closed! It's – it's like the promised land, it's right there, you can see the lights are still on and the guy is mopping the floor, there's somebody in there who could help me out, and I'm pounding on the door, he's like, get out of here, man, I'm going no no no you can't turn me away, you got to save me, dude! I'm truly, I'm pounding on the door –

LORNA. You were pounding on the door?

JACK. Guy's going like, go away go away, I'm yelling – polite, but forceful – I'm yelling YOU GOT TO SELL ME SOME ICE CREAM, MAN! COME SAVE ME YOU MOTHERFUCKER!

(laughing)

This guy is, I'm calling the police, I'm going no no don't call the cops COME ON.

(laughing)

It was fucking surreal.

LORNA. Did he call the police?

JACK. No, he sold me ice cream. How do you think I got this stuff? The guy opened the door and sold it to me.

LORNA. That was nice of him.

JACK. I paid him a thousand bucks for it. I wouldn't call it a huge fucking favor. But we both walked away satisfied, which doesn't always happen, I'll say that.

LORNA. You paid him a thousand dollars? For ice cream?

JACK. Yes I did that's right I did. You know what, as good as this is, I have to say I like the black raspberry better.

(He finds a different carton.)

LORNA. Does Jenny know you're here?

JACK. No. No, no, I would say, no.

LORNA. Did something happen?

JACK. What? Like what, like did I kill her or something?

LORNA. *(startled)* Did you?

JACK. *(laughing)* Did I kill my wife? Hello!

LORNA. Well why did you say that?

JACK. *(laughing)* Because you were looking at me like I killed her! Which maybe I might want to kill her? But no. She's fine. She knows how to take care of herself, my lovely wife. She's great.

LORNA. You're an asshole. Did you two have a fight or something?

JACK. Yeah, 'or something.' Hey hey hey caramel. That was always your drug of choice, wasn't it?

(He hands it to her.)

LORNA. Yes, caramel is my favorite, but I don't want any right now, thanks.

JACK. Why not?

LORNA. I'm on a diet.

JACK. Why?

LORNA. To lose weight.

JACK. You don't need to lose weight.

LORNA. Well I'd like to lose weight.

JACK. Yeah but why? You know, I just have to tell you, everybody in New York is too skinny. The women are all, they look so unhappy! Their figures are nice, but their faces are unhappy. People in the Midwest are not unhappy.

LORNA. Oh course they are.

JACK. Not really.

LORNA. They're miserable.

JACK. Not compared to the sociopaths who live in New York. Compared to New Yorkers people here are peaceful and content.

LORNA. People here are mean and stupid.

JACK. Not the guy at Graeter's. He's pretty happy.

LORNA. Yeah, because you gave him a thousand bucks.

JACK. That's right, I did. That guy is going to feel fantastic for days.

LORNA. So what happened basically is he got a thousand bucks, which he pocketed, and then he let you take as much ice cream as you wanted.

JACK. The free market is a beautiful thing.

LORNA. That's not the free market. That's stealing.

JACK. I paid.

LORNA. You didn't pay Graeters.

JACK. They'll never know.

LORNA. That makes it all right?

JACK. You'd be surprised.

LORNA. You know what? I think, this is, what you did is immoral. I think that.

JACK. Immoral?

LORNA. Yeah. You paid that guy to be corrupt.

JACK. *(laughing)* 'Corrupt?'

LORNA. Yes.

JACK. I gave him a thousand bucks! You know how much Graeter's is paying him, to mop their floors at eleven thirty at night?

LORNA. Not very much, I'm sure. But –

JACK. Yeah, I'm sure too. And he was not a young guy. He was working his ass off. He probably holds down three jobs just to pay his mortgage, if he still has one. Maybe he has a wife, maybe he has kids. He was working hard. Someone hands him a thousand dollars, that's a good thing. This was an awesome day for that guy. I'm a fucking hero, to that guy.

LORNA. Because you got him to take a bribe. You bribed him to steal for you.

(A beat. He looks at her.)

JACK. You know what? You're right. You do, you look unhappy.

LORNA. I'm not unhappy.

JACK. So you say, but you look pretty fucking unhappy.

LORNA. Jack, what are you doing here?

JACK. I live here!

LORNA. Mom and Dad live here.

JACK. And you too, right?

LORNA. Yes, I live here; for now I live here. What are you doing here?

JACK. *(a shrug)* I grew up here.

LORNA. So?

JACK. So, that means it's always my home.

LORNA. Have you run that one by mom and dad? Because I think they'll be a bit startled to hear it.

JACK. Really? Because I think they'll just, be happy. I'm their son. I've come home. I think that will make them happy. I don't think they'll care why. I think they'll be happy.

(She thinks about this. Toys with a carton of ice cream.)

No. No. This one's the caramel.

(He shoves it toward her. Hands her a spoon. After a moment, she takes a bite.)

See? Aren't you happy?

(Blackout.)

Scene Two

(The following morning. **BARBARA,** *Jack and Lorna's mother, is looking in the freezer.* **LORNA** *is on the phone.)*

LORNA. No, he didn't, he didn't –

(beat)

Well, he –

(beat)

No. I don't –

(beat)

Honestly, Sharon, I don't know he – I don't know. I don't know. SHARON. I don't KNOW.

(beat)

I'm not yelling I'm just trying to tell you –

(beat)

No.

(beat)

No. I don't know.

(beat)

I don't know.

(beat)

I don't know.

(beat)

Look, I got to go. Yeah, sorry, I really have to go. See you.

(hangs up)

I hate her.

BARBARA. You two never got along.

LORNA. Yeah, because she's a bitch.

BARBARA. You could be a little nicer.

LORNA. Why don't you tell her to be nicer?

BARBARA. Because I'm not talking to her; I'm talking to you.

LORNA. Do you ever tell her to be nicer? Do you ever say, Sharon, maybe you could stop bossing Lorna around and just be nice to her once in a while?

BARBARA. You should both be nicer.

LORNA. SHE should be nicer.

BARBARA. But you could be nicer now.

LORNA. I don't want to be nicer!

BARBARA. Then why did you call her?

LORNA. Because you told me to!

(She screams with frustration.)

BARBARA. You're going to wake up your father and he needs his sleep; he's not been sleeping well at all.

LORNA. He's out, Mom, those painkillers knock him out.

BARBARA. He's taking too many of those things. I'm not talking about how much they cost. I'm talking about oxygen. Your blood oxygen plummets. And he's had pneumonia twice this year. You can't breath, it settles in your lungs. I'm not talking about the cost. I can take a job at Krogers or Florsheim's, that wouldn't kill me, that's not –

LORNA. *(overlap)* Mom, no one thinks –

BARBARA. That's not what its about. It's not about the bills. It's about oxygen. Breathing. He should just learn to put up with the pain. It's good for you.

LORNA. Pain is not good for you! That is a Catholic myth that pain is good for you.

BARBARA. It's better than not being able to breathe.

LORNA. He's got kidney stones, Mom, they're awful, they hurt, and he has to take that stuff while he's passing them. I talked to the doctor a bunch of times about it and he says kidney stones are just the worst.

BARBARA. Dying, is the worst.

LORNA. You know what, you know who you should talk to about this, is Jack. Jack honestly had a lot of opinions about painkillers last night. He seemed to know a lot about them.

BARBARA. Did he say, you shouldn't take too many?

LORNA. I don't think that's actually his position, no.

BARBARA. Well what did he say?

LORNA. He just seemed very knowledgeable.

BARBARA. And he just showed up? Out of the blue?

LORNA. Yes, I told you, that's what happened. He walked through the door, with a lot of ice cream and he seemed a little uptight.

BARBARA. He was always high strung.

LORNA. Even for him, he was pretty high strung.

BARBARA. Well what was he doing?

LORNA. He was eating ice cream and you know, saying things.

BARBARA. What things?

LORNA. I don't know, it was very a lot. You know how he can be a lot. A lot of observations about the world and things like that.

BARBARA. He was always so smart. Even when he was little. So quick.

LORNA. Yes.

BARBARA. Really just brilliant. You were never brilliant. But you did, you worked hard.

LORNA. Yeah, thanks.

BARBARA. But Jack!

LORNA. I'm aware.

BARBARA. And Jenny didn't come with him?

LORNA. No, no Jenny.

BARBARA. Did he say why not?

LORNA. I didn't ask.

BARBARA. Why not?

LORNA. Because I don't like Jenny and it's more fun when she's not here.

BARBARA. You don't like anybody.

LORNA. You don't like Jenny either, Mom!

BARBARA. I don't mind her. I just think she's cold. And it worries me, that she has no belief.

LORNA. Jack has no belief either.

BARBARA. So you tell me.

LORNA. So Jack tells you. Don't put this on me! I got no problem with God. I believe in God.

BARBARA. You don't go to church.

LORNA. I believe in God and I don't believe in church. A lot of people hold this position.

BARBARA. People who are kidding themselves.

LORNA. Mom do you really want to get into this right now?

BARBARA. Is there a better time?

LORNA. After breakfast would be a better time.

BARBARA. You know when I was a girl, I went to Mass six days a week. Of course on Sunday but Monday through Friday as well, it was a part of our school day. And on the Holy Days, Ash Wednesday and Good Friday, we would be in church all afternoon. Which wasn't easy, let me tell you. On your knees for hours, with all the incense from the altar. A lot of kids fainted. They'd just fall right over.

LORNA. Mom. This doesn't make church sound like fun.

BARBARA. It wasn't fun.

LORNA. Well, why would I want to go?

BARBARA. You didn't want to go. You had to go.

LORNA. Yeah but I don't have to go.

BARBARA. I know that's the position your generation wants to take.

LORNA. Mom seriously. How did we get here? I'm not awake yet. I was up late with Jack, eating ice cream, and mostly I am still thinking about that and how I was doing so well on my diet and I ate a whole pint of caramel ice cream in the middle of the night and wrecked everything. That's really what I'm thinking about.

BARBARA. Religion can be a great comfort.

LORNA. Yeah, let me tell you something, Mom. That story you just told about the little kids keeling over? That's not a comforting story. To a lot of people, "comfort" is not what we think of when we think of the word "Catholic."

BARBARA. It centers you. It gives you common ground. Maybe while he's here, I can see if Jack wants to come to church with me.

LORNA. That's a fantastic idea. I think you should tell Jack that as soon as he gets up, that you think he should go to church with you. Do it before he's had any coffee.

BARBARA. Well I know you're being sarcastic, but I will... Maybe we should call Jenny.

(She goes to get the phone.)

LORNA. Call Jenny, why?

BARBARA. To find out what's going on with Jack!

LORNA. Why don't you ask Jack what's going on with Jack?

BARBARA. Well I will but a little extra information never hurt anybody. You should call her.

(She gives **LORNA** *the phone.)*

LORNA. I am not calling Jenny. If you want to talk to her, you call her.

BARBARA. Oh, she's not going to talk to me. She has always made it very clear, how she feels about me. You call her.

LORNA. I'm not calling her.

(She pushes the phone to **BARBARA**.*)*

BARBARA. Well I guess that's up to you.

LORNA. Yes it is up to me, and I'm not going to call her.

*(***BARBARA** *sighs.)*

What? What?

BARBARA. I just don't think it's a very helpful position.

(The phone rings. **LORNA** *answers it.)*

LORNA. Hello. Oh hi Doug. I'm so glad you called.

(to **BARBARA***)*

It's Doug.

(on phone)

Yeah, Jack's here.

BARBARA. *(overlap)* Oh it's Doug I want to talk to him.

LORNA. *(ignoring her, talking to* **DOUG***)* No, he didn't, he just showed up last night. *(to* **BARBARA***:)* Mom, I'm talking!

BARBARA. *(overlap)* He wanted to know if I knew of anyone looking for work as a house cleaner. *(to* **LORNA***:)* I know!

LORNA. *(overlap)* No kidding he like just walked in the door, with this huge bag of ice cream, he had like eight pints of Graeters and this crazy story. Oh my God.

BARBARA. *(continue overlap)* Janet Newman's daughter-in-law says her person is really good and she isn't sure if she does cooking, which Diane said that was what she was looking for, someone who can both cook and clean.

(She goes to a counter and starts to look for a paper.)

LORNA. *(overlap)* I don't know. He was just talking in circles.

BARBARA. *(overlap, she's found the number)* I don't know what he's thinking, honestly, it's not like Diane is working full time, and she does nothing, the house is a wreck and now she doesn't even want to do the cooking, I don't think her paycheck will even cover the cost of the extra help but they don't want to hear my opinion about it.

LORNA. *(overlap)* No, Mom and Dad were asleep, he was pretty loud you know how he can be, but Dad's on so much Percoset right now he is just OUT and Mom fell asleep with the television on up there, she's been watching the news incessantly lately or not watching it, as the case may be because it just knocks her right out and I have to go up there and turn it off for her.

(*JACK* enters. *BARBARA* *is getting herself coffee and doesn't see him.*)

Honestly it's insane around here and who knows what is up with Jack.

BARBARA. Both my sons married horrible women. There. I said it.

JACK. Mom?

BARBARA. Oh Jack. Good morning, sweetheart I didn't know you were up.

JACK. Mom.

(*He goes to her, kneels before her and hugs her.* *BARBARA* *doesn't know what to do.* *LORNA* *watches this. Then, to phone:*)

LORNA. I got to go.

(*She hangs up.*)

JACK. You were right. I should have stayed here. I should have stayed in Cincinnati.

(*He continues to hug her, on his knees.*)

LORNA. What are you doing? Would you get up?

(*She pries him loose and helps him stand.*)

JACK. Too much? Perhaps. On the other hand, why the hell not? She's my mother. Why not show a little appreciation once in a while? Jesus it's a gorgeous day. Look at this. You look out the back window, that's incredible. You know what they don't have in New York? Trees. Seriously. I mean there are some trees, like in Central Park, and in Brooklyn, somewhere, but you can go for BLOCKS in Midtown, the Financial District – and you have to ask yourself – I have to ask myself – whose idiotic idea was THAT? To get rid of the TREES? You know what else we have here, that they don't have there? Air. Like, air, you can breathe, they don't have any of that, anymore. Seriously, you can't live there. I'm so happy to be here! I feel so much better already. You know what? Lorna, you know what? You look fantastic.

(He kisses her on the cheek.)

Good morning. You look so pretty. You too, Mom.

BARBARA. Thank you, sweetheart.

LORNA. Jack guess what, Mom has a big idea. Mom, tell Jack your big idea.

BARBARA. It's fine.

LORNA. No, it's a good idea. I really do think it's a terrific idea.

BARBARA. I know what you think.

LORNA. She wants you to go to church with her.

JACK. Church? Like, God church?

BARBARA. You used to love going to church. When you were little, you were so cute in those altar boy robes. You loved it! Helping Father Conlin, with the censor, and the chalice.

LORNA. Yeah, especially the chalice. That guy was a total alcoholic.

BARBARA. We all know how you felt about it. You didn't respect authority.

LORNA. I didn't respect alcoholics.

BARBARA. Girls weren't supposed to be altar boys. You just never accepted that. You always wanted things you couldn't have.

LORNA. Lots of people want things that they can't have, Mom. It's not a sin.

JACK. It is, actually. Coveting thy neighbor's goods.

LORNA. Wanting to be an altar boy doesn't count as a sin!

JACK. It totally counts as a sin! It's the biggest sin out there! Witch!

BARBARA. Girls cannot be altar boys.

LORNA. They can. Now they're all over! Some of them have dreadlocks!

BARBARA. I know. It's terrible.

LORNA. It's not terrible. I wanted to do it. They let him do it. It looked like fun to me.

JACK. Please. You just wanted to get on that altar so you could menstruate up there.

LORNA. *(laughing)* Hey wait hey wait, do you remember, remember that midnight mass when there was that harp up there, with a cover on it, and you said it looked like a dead angel and then we couldn't stop laughing.

JACK. *(laughing)* Oh my God and Sharon was all – "you guys" –

LORNA. *(snotty voice)* "This is a holy place."

BARBARA. I don't remember this.

JACK. You were there, everybody was there – "you guys" – "I'm appalled!"

LORNA. And Dad, he was the worst.

JACK. We'd finally all calm down and then he'd go "dead angel – "

(They both start to laugh harder.)

BARBARA. I don't remember.

JACK. You were there.

BARBARA. There are whole years I don't remember. Six kids. Whole years just disappear.

JACK. "Dead angel."

(They snicker and burst out laughing. BARBARA sighs)

BARBARA. Okay. You can laugh. But I agree with Sharon, Mass is a holy place. And I really do think that prayer can lead you to a deeper truth.

JACK. Well, that sounds awesome. I would love that, Mom.

BARBARA. Would you?

JACK. Absolutely. Deeper truth, who wouldn't want that?

BARBARA. Then you'll come to church with me?

JACK. Sure.

LORNA. You're going to go to church. To like Mass. With Mom.

JACK. Why not. How's dad feeling?

(JACK *goes to the freezer and takes out ice cream, starts to eat it.*)

BARBARA. Not so great.

JACK. Well we have to do something about that. So it's kidney stones again? How many times has he been through this?

BARBARA. I don't know. It's constant. Now they're talking about kidney failure and he's had pneumonia twice, already. In one year! It's horrible, being old, don't get me started.

JACK. We need to get him some better doctors. So who is the best urologist in Cincinnati?

LORNA. Are you asking me?

JACK. I'm asking anybody.

BARBARA. The doctor he has is fine.

JACK. Doctor's are not supposed to be fine, Mom. You need the best one.

BARBARA. We're on Medicare, we're not allowed to pick our own doctor.

JACK. You can if you pay for it.

(*He pulls a wad of bills out of his pocket, holds it up, and drops it on the table. He goes to the phone, picks it up.*)

So who do we know might be able to help us out with a referral?

LORNA. What is that?

JACK. It's money.

LORNA. How much money?

JACK. How much do you need?

LORNA. Where did you get it?

JACK. I stole it.

   (beat)

   I'm kidding! It's mine. It's mine.

   (laughing)

   Seriously! It's mine. So let's call this doctor.

   *(He picks up the phone. **BARBARA** and **LORNA** look at the wad of bills on the table.)*

   (Blackout.)

Scene Three

(The following night. JACK *is opening beers.* PHIL *sits at the table. There are bags of Skyline Chili piled on the table.)*

PHIL. This is a lot of chili.

JACK. Don't blame me, man. I've been in the desert a long time. What do you want?

PHIL. Cheese coney?

JACK. Cheese coney!

PHIL. Yeah, a cheese coney would be great.

*(*JACK *shoves some bags at him.)*

JACK. Help yourself. I think I got like fifty.

PHIL. Really?

JACK. Well Jesus, they're so cheap. Ridiculous. You know, you could eat thousands of cheese coneys for the cost of one dinner at Babbo. And that's literally true, I mean I am not exaggerating or being metaphorical here.

PHIL. What's a Babbo?

JACK. Right? I mean, precisely. I mean, it's, you know, in New York, people eat like, you can go to a deli, or some vendor on a street corner and it's all right, you know, that's not bad, for just like food that you need to eat fast to keep yourself going for the next ten hours.

You can do that there. Or, you go to some place like just some – places that are, the food is incredible in New York. Steaks that you can't, there is no, there are steaks that I have eaten that I dream about to this day, that I ate, in New York. Italian restaurants in New York are better than Italian restaurants anywhere else in the world, including Italy. And I do not say that lightly. I'm not talking about pussy food. I'm talking about meals that go on for hours, or days. One time I went to a dinner party, you had to walk down three flights of stairs – I'm talking down, into the earth, on subterranean passageways under a lake, past an underground forest – no, I'm shitting you about the lake and the forest but seriously, you had to go down these stairs and through the kitchen and into a like hidden room down there, used to be a speakeasy, and then it was a wine cellar and now it's like this hidden room and there was a dinner party, down there, under the city, duck breast on a red wine reduction with shallots and fennel confit, the thing was, plus someone stood up and sang opera, seriously, one of the people at this dinner party was a guest artist with the Met or something and he stood up and sang this fucking Puccini aria, the waiters were hovering by the doors to listen, the whole earth was silent. That's the kind of thing that happens around food, in New York. And it doesn't come close to a cheese coney. It just doesn't.

PHIL. *(beat)* Still, that sounds pretty great.

JACK. It was okay.

PHIL. He was like an opera singer?

JACK. Apparently.

PHIL. Underground? That, like, really happened?

JACK. Everything I say is true.

PHIL. Really?

JACK. Seriously. You know, when you hit that point, where there's just no point, to even talk if you're not telling the truth? You know that point?

PHIL. I'm not... sure.

JACK. Good. Good for you, man. Don't lay your cards out all over the table for people to piss on them. You're smart, don't give anything up. Fuck it. Right? Fuck it.

PHIL. Right.

JACK. You were always smarter than me.

PHIL. Maybe not so much.

JACK. You stayed here. I mean, you knew, right? I remember. I was all, come on man there's a whole world out there and you didn't fall for it. You just, you were coherent.

PHIL. Coherent, I don't know.

JACK. You knew who you were. It wasn't all, Jesus, the rest of us, running around like fucking lunatics.

PHIL. Oh my God. You ever hear from –

JACK. Nobody. I don't hear from anybody.

PHIL. That's too bad.

JACK. Nobody.

PHIL. I see some people. Jay Durrwhachter moved back something like six years ago, he moved his whole family back and he took over his father's you know. Chrysler dealership.

JACK. I don't remember him.

PHIL. Jay Durrwachter? He had sort of brown hair, glasses, he played the trombone in the jazz band?

JACK. No.

PHIL. Well he's here now. Let's see. John Walker? He's on the west coast but sometimes I see him, his mom is in a home here. He calls sometimes, when he comes through. Who else? Oh. Mark Toobin.

JACK. I hated that guy.

PHIL. Yeah. He lives here now.

JACK. What an asshole.

PHIL. Sometimes I play tennis with him. He's better now, than he was.

JACK. He was a total asshole.

PHIL. He's better now.

(beat)

It's great that you called.

JACK. Of course I called.

PHIL. No, it's been a while.

JACK. Totally. I totally will be better now.

PHIL. No, come on. People move away, you get used to it.

(beat)

That's a great suit.

JACK. Oh, yeah. Thanks.

PHIL. What kind of suit is that?

JACK. Armani.

PHIL. Wow. An Armani suit! Somebody said you made a lot of money.

JACK. In New York, there's a lot of money to be made.

PHIL. But it's expensive there too.

JACK. That's not the worst thing to be said about New York. Although the dry cleaning bills do make you wonder.

PHIL. *(looking around)* So your wife's not with you?

JACK. *(laughing)* No. That is, actually, no. She's not with me.

PHIL. Is that funny?

JACK. In a kind of gallows humor way, you would have to say yes. I mean, don't get me wrong. It's not like I killed her.

PHIL. I didn't think that.

JACK. Listen, check this out. Check this out. She's old money. She's old everything. You don't notice it right away, because she's so young and beautiful, but everything else is old. Her mother's wedding dress. They remake it every time someone gets married, so that your wife still looks hot in it, but it's old. Dad's apartment? Old. The house in East Hampton. Old. The family itself is so fucking old they're older than America. This is true.

PHIL. Everything you say...

JACK. That's right. They are so old, that they have relics. From England.

PHIL. Relics?

JACK. Yes. Relics.

PHIL. Wow.

JACK. And one of these relics, is a teapot.

PHIL. A tea pot?

JACK. Yeah, like a silver tea pot. From England. It came over with them on the Mayflower. It is a Mayflower teapot.

PHIL. Really?

JACK. Yes. And this Mayflower teapot was given to me and my bride on our wedding day. It was our present. It was my welcome to the family present.

PHIL. That's cool.

JACK. So we're dividing the property, right? And things are – shit, they're, she's – it's, so I say, you know what? If it's going to be like this? You're going after me like this? Communal property, no prenup, no marriage, everything just gone, like worse than gone, like you have to punish me for ever thinking, fuck you, then that fucking teapot is part of the communal property. Right? The Mayflower teapot, that belongs to both of us! They gave it, to both of us!

PHIL. *(cautious)* Yeah?

JACK. Only check this out. No one knows where it is. It's been in the vault, right, at the bank, since the wedding? It's just not there anymore. It's just gone. Mysteriously. Out of the BANK. Now, things disappear from banks. Nobody knows that better than me, how that can happen. But not a Mayflower teapot.

(beat)

PHIL. Okay, I'm a little confused.

JACK. I'm not.

(LORNA enters from upstairs.)

LORNA. Okay I'm going to kill her. I'm not kidding Jack you have to go up there. She's driving me crazy.

PHIL. *(smitten)* Hi, Lorna.

LORNA. *(not noticing)* Hey Phil. Oh, for crying out loud. Would you look at this! What, you guys stop by Skyline, pick up a little snack?

PHIL. You want a cheese coney?

LORNA. Okay I would love a cheese coney but Jack honestly this is nuts! We still have all that ice cream. And I'm serious, you have to go up there and talk to her. He's passing a fucking kidney stone and she's hidden the

Percoset. Would you tell her? Tell her, that he needs those things, the pain could kill him.

(to PHIL*)*

Did he tell you, she's got some crazy fixation now, that painkillers are bad for your blood oxygen and she thinks he's going to die, if he has too many.

PHIL. That's actually true.

LORNA. Could you please not tell her that? He's been so sick for so long. He's had the kidney stones eight times now. Eight. It's not his diet, he hardly eats anything anymore. So it's something wrong with the kidneys, they just can't tell you what.

JACK. Here, give him some of these.

(He reaches into his pocket and pulls out a prescription bottle, hands it to her.)

(She looks at it.)

LORNA. What is it?

JACK. Trust me. It won't cure his kidney stones, but he will be reconciled.

LORNA. Why don't you go up there. He would like to see you.

JACK. I don't think he would.

(She sighs.)

LORNA. And these things won't kill him, right?

JACK. No.

(beat)

Are you kidding? You think I want to kill my own father? Oh that would be good for my psyche. That would really help settle things down. Let's just add that one, to my list of sins.

LORNA. What is your list of sins?

JACK. *(laughing)* You know what? You can sit there, and finish your cheese coney, and poke at me. Or you could do a big big favor, for our dad. Go on. I'm not kidding. Those pills are magic.

LORNA. Magic pills. I can't believe I'm even considering this.

JACK. *(simple)* They'll make him feel a lot better.

(*She looks at him, believes him, and goes.* PHIL *and* JACK *look at each other.*)

Okay talk to me, you fucking loser. You still have a crush on my sister?

PHIL. I don't have a crush on –

JACK. You are so in love, you're pathetic. Is that why you came over here?

PHIL. I came because you asked me, you called me –

JACK. You're retarded.

PHIL. Okay.

JACK. She's getting old. Ask her out.

PHIL. I'm not going to ask her out.

JACK. Why not? She's still pretty. She's old, but pretty. And you're not a big stud anymore. If you ever were. If you think you're going to get some young hot porn star –

PHIL. I don't want a young hot porno star!

JACK. Then what's wrong with Lorna? Okay. She seems like a loser, a little bit, because she's living at home with her parents but that's just circumstance. She wasted a lot of years on a total bonehead –

PHIL. Craig Bueller –

JACK. That's right Craig the bonehead but it's because she was loyal. She was very loyal to someone who didn't deserve it, and now she's here, taking care of our aging parents, these are fine qualities in a person. She's great.

PHIL. I know!

JACK. And what have you been doing? What makes you so great? After high school you did nothing!

PHIL. I didn't do nothing!

JACK. You stayed in Cincinnati –

PHIL. I like it here!

JACK. You never tested yourself. You never pushed yourself.

PHIL. Look, could you just –

JACK. You're just not such hot shit. You could ask my sister out. It wouldn't kill you.

PHIL. I did ask her out and she wasn't interested.

JACK. You did?

PHIL. Yes.

JACK. You asked her out.

PHIL. Yes, I did.

JACK. I didn't know that.

PHIL. Well, I did. Senior year. I asked her out. She wasn't interested.

(beat)

JACK. You asked her out senior year?

PHIL. Yeah.

JACK. That was fifteen fucking years ago, you fucking loser! She only gets one shot every fifteen years?

PHIL. She said –

JACK. I don't give a shit what she said! You're going to ask her again. When she comes back down I'm going to make an excuse and give you a minute to just talk to her, say hi, tell her she looks pretty, and ask her out.

PHIL. I don't –

JACK. We're not arguing about this. You're going to do it.

(There is a beat. Both of them take a bite of their cheese coneys. They eat.)

PHIL. I'm sorry to hear about your divorce.

JACK. It's okay.

PHIL. No, I am, I'm really sorry.

(A beat. LORNA reenters, from upstairs.)

LORNA. Okay. I gave him those pills. They better not kill him.

JACK. How many did you give him?

LORNA. Two.

JACK. *(startled, horrified)* Two? You gave him two?

LORNA. Yeah, why?

JACK. You are so gullible.

(JACK laughs at her.)

LORNA. You're a jerk.

(She takes a bite of her cheese coney.)

JACK. I'm going to go get some beer.

LORNA. What are you talking about, we have beer.

JACK. This isn't beer. This is like light beer, there's no beer in this beer. I'm going to go get something with a little testosterone in it.

LORNA. What, you mean you're going to go drive away and get some?

JACK. Yes, I'm going to the King Kwick, and get a real beer! This is the Midwest, there's a real beer out there somewhere, and I'm going to go find it. Hudepohl! I'm gonna get some Hoodie!

(He goes. LORNA looks at PHIL, startled.)

LORNA. Did he just leave?

PHIL. I think so.

LORNA. Oh, for crying out loud. He just left. He invited you over for dinner, and now he's leaving?

PHIL. He just went to get beer.

LORNA. No, I know, I just – seriously, he's been acting so nuts. Like, okay he clearly can afford to buy sixteen thousand cheese coneys, but is that any reason to do it?

PHIL. It's really only about ten, I think.

LORNA. Yeah but why would you need to buy ten cheese coneys?

PHIL. When we were in high school, we could actually eat ten cheese coneys. A piece. I think I did, once. And, you know. He thought you might want one. Or your mom.

LORNA. Last night, he – I can't even tell you what he did last night. It was kind of illegal.

PHIL. Really?

LORNA. I mean nobody got hurt. He did this thing at Graeter's, the one up on Kenwood Road?

PHIL. Yeah?

LORNA. I can't tell you. It's maybe worse than I think. It's fine. I'm sure it's fine.

PHIL. I'm sure it is.

(then)

It's great to see you. You look so pretty. You look fantastic.

LORNA. Oh please. I'm a mess. And now I'm eating a cheese coney. Last night I ate an entire PINT of Graeter's ice cream. I mean I'm glad to see him, I am, but this has been a disaster for my diet.

PHIL. You don't need to lose weight.

LORNA. Yes but I want to lose weight. I want to lose a few pounds!

PHIL. But you don't need to. You look so pretty.

LORNA. I can't have this much junk food around when I'm under so much stress because then you know, you eat it. Cheese coneys. Jesus CHRIST these things are delicious. Get this thing away from me! Wait.

(She takes a bite out of it and gives it to him.)

PHIL. I love cheese coneys.

LORNA. *(mouth full)* Me too but I'm getting so fat –

PHIL. I don't think you're fat at all.

LORNA. Oh God. Oh God. That was so delicious.

(He smiles. He really is happy with this.)

PHIL. So. You know. Listen.

LORNA. I mean, when he showed up out of the blue like that – I did, my first thought was, thank God! Sharon is useless and Doug and Karen and Beth are all wrapped up in their kids, and I'm like – just alone here. And I did I thought thank God, someone is here to help me! But this is, I think something's wrong. You don't think he's on drugs, do you? He must be on drugs, he's carrying drugs around with him. But those things are pain killers. They're not crystal meth or anything.

PHIL. Would he do that?

LORNA. No. No. He wouldn't. I don't know what he'd do. He's different. New York made him different.

PHIL. No.

LORNA. I think there's something wrong. I think he's in trouble. I think something's wrong.

(She starts to cry.)

PHIL. Oh. God.

LORNA. Sorry.

PHIL. No –

(He touches her shoulder. She turns her head.)

LORNA. I'm sorry.

PHIL. He's fine.

LORNA. He's not fine!

PHIL. He's just high strung.

LORNA. That's what my mom says.

PHIL. She's right. Your mom is more right than you think.

LORNA. That doesn't seem possible.

PHIL. He's going through something, clearly.

LORNA. Yes.

PHIL. But we all are.

LORNA. Are we?

PHIL. Yes! You know, getting older. Life. It's not what we thought.

LORNA. No, it's not.

PHIL. And he's feeling that right now. That's why he came home. He's come back here, to center himself. To focus. To remember who he is.

LORNA. Did he tell you that?

PHIL. Not specifically, but isn't that what you sense?

LORNA. It is, actually. That's what I was thinking.

PHIL. I think you should trust your instincts. You love him.

LORNA. I do.

PHIL. Then, you should trust him.

LORNA. I do!

PHIL. He's just going through something. The divorce I think really has him kind of shaken up.

(She looks at him. He smiles at her. A beat.)

Listen. Would you – like, maybe want to –

LORNA. Hang on. Hang on. What divorce?

PHIL. The divorce. His divorce.

LORNA. *(pissed)* He's getting a divorce?

(A beat. Blackout.)

Scene Four

(The next morning. **LORNA** *is on the phone.* **BARBARA**
is making toast.)

LORNA. So he didn't tell you either.

(to **BARBARA***)*

Beth says she didn't know either.

BARBARA. Oh is that Beth?

LORNA. *(on phone)* No, I haven't talked to Doug yet but I
called Karen and he didn't tell her or me or mom.

BARBARA. *(overlap)* Tell her I haven't sent the package for
Emily.

*(She goes into the next room and returns a moment later
with an open box, filled with stuff.)*

LORNA. No, he told Phil it was happening, like they're way
down the road.

BARBARA. *(overlap)* I had it all ready to go and your father
was going to mail it last week, and then this thing with
the kidney stones started, and then we were back and
forth from the hospital for two days –

LORNA. *(overlap)* It was so embarrassing to hear about it
that way. *(to* **BARBARA***:)* Mom, I'm talking!

BARBARA. I know!

LORNA. *(overlap)* Phil was completely mortified that he
was the one who told me because Jack apparently just
tossed it out there like it was common knowledge.

BARBARA. *(overlap)* Ask her if she wants you to take it to
the UPS office, that might get it there a little sooner,
I guess you could do that.

LORNA. Phil, you know, Phil Gunstler, Jack's friend from
kindergarten or high school, he still lives here and –
yes you do. He asked me out once, junior year, but I
couldn't go because I had band camp that weekend
and then he never asked me again and I was so mad,
like that's it, all I get is one try? I'm still mad about it.

BARBARA. *(overlap)* Oh, if Beth wants to return it, that's okay, but she only has thirty days. I'm putting the receipt in with it. Or I can keep it here. Whatever she prefers.

LORNA. *(overlap)* Yeah, right? No, he's not up yet. If I find out anything I'll call you.

(She hangs up.)

So Beth didn't know either. None of us knew. I'm so mad at him.

(JACK enters on this, sleepy and befuddled.)

JACK. Who, who are you mad at?

LORNA. You, you jerk.

JACK. *(yawning)* Is there coffee? Ice cream, is there coffee ice cream. Hey, Mom, you look so pretty.

(He goes to the freezer and starts to look through it.)

LORNA. *(hostile)* Good morning, sleepy head.

JACK. Good morning to you, angry girl.

(then)

What's she mad about?

BARBARA. Well, Jack, you should have told us.

JACK. Told you what?

LORNA. That one little matter? That just slipped your mind?

(He is awake now, and alert. He turns to look at **LORNA.** *)*

JACK. I got a lot going on in the old cranium, lot of balls in the air, sometimes the occasional detail does escape my attention. So what detail, in particular, are we talking about?

(beat)

LORNA. The divorce?

JACK. The divorce. The divorce!

(a relief, dawning)

Phil told you –

LORNA. Yes, he did! You and Jenny are getting a divorce?

JACK. Yes, we are. Jenny and I are getting a divorce.

LORNA. Well, he made it sound like, this has been happening for a while, like you're well down the line, like you've been in the middle of this for months and months and months!

JACK. What is the big deal? You never liked Jenny. You told me not to marry her.

LORNA. I did not.

JACK. Yes you did! Maybe Beth did. Or Karen. It wasn't Doug, it was one of the girls. Christ Mom you had too many girls, I cannot keep them straight. And then naming two of them Sharon and Karen, that was almost malicious, frankly.

BARBARA. Well, that was your father's idea.

LORNA. I never said you shouldn't marry her.

JACK. Well, I don't care who was the one who actually said it. You all hated Jenny on sight.

BARBARA. I did not! I liked her!

JACK. Ha.

BARBARA. I just wondered, if she was warm.

JACK. No she was not warm. Warm is not what she was.

(He sits, eating ice cream.)

(beat)

LORNA. Was?

JACK. Yes, was. I killed her, she's dead now, she was alive but now she's dead.

(A horrible pause. He laughs.)

LORNA. Jack would you stop saying things like that!

JACK. *(laughing)* Was! Was, she's not my wife anymore, or at least she's almost not my wife. Back then she was my wife, but she wasn't warm back then, or now either, I'm afraid. Was. She was a piece of work, and she still is a piece of work, but I'm not in that, anymore. So. That's what "was."

LORNA. Why didn't you tell us?

JACK. Tell you what? That you were right about her? That all my sisters, and my mother, were right about my wife, that she was not warm, and I should not have married her? Yeah, okay. I should have told you. Sorry.

(He's not.)

BARBARA. Well, it's just very sad, and we're sorry to hear it.

JACK. Okay.

BARBARA. I probably should call her.

JACK. Yeah, no you shouldn't.

BARBARA. Jack, we have to acknowledge. That we're sorry.

JACK. I already told her that we're sorry. I, in particular, am very, very sorry.

BARBARA. I just think that someone, that one of us, one of the family, should acknowledge the loss.

JACK. That's very sweet and Midwestern of you, Mom, but trust me, it's not necessary. She never liked you either.

BARBARA. She didn't, well I knew that. She has never been shy about letting me know that.

JACK. That's right. So you don't need to call her.

BARBARA. She was a member of this family for seven years.

JACK. And now that long, horrible nightmare is over. Trust me. You don't have to call her.

LORNA. It's fine, Mom. I already did it.

JACK. You did what?

LORNA. I called Jenny. To say we're sorry. So you don't have to do it, Mom. I did it.

JACK. You called Jenny.

LORNA. Yes Jack, after your old friend Phil told me, your sister, about your divorce, I called her because I thought it was really rude that you never told us and even though none of us ever liked her someone from the family should say sorry to hear about the divorce! So whether or not it's too sweet or Midwestern it doesn't matter. It's already done.

JACK. You called her.

LORNA. Yes I did, you lunatic. I wanted to make sure that you hadn't killed her, so I called her last night to make sure she was all right!

JACK. But you didn't talk to her.

LORNA. No I left a message.

JACK. And you said I was here?

LORNA. I can't remember what I said.

JACK. Could you try?

(The doorbell rings.)

BARBARA. I'll get it.

JACK. No don't don't don't.

(beat)

Sorry. Sorry. Go ahead.

(BARBARA looks at him, then goes. JACK laughs a little to himself, shrugs.)

LORNA. What is going on, Jack?

JACK. *(a breath, then)* You know, you really are great. Phil still has a huge crush on you, in case you're interested. Not that it has to be Phil. But it has to be something, Lorna. You can't hide at home forever. Where you're going to needs to be the place you want to be.

LORNA. What are you talking about?

JACK. It's complicated. But anything true, is!

(BARBARA enters.)

BARBARA. Jack? Guess who's here!

(JENNY enters. She is gorgeous and stylish, cold and well dressed. It is as if New York itself just walked into the room.)

JENNY. Hello, Jack.

JACK. Hi, honey.

LORNA. Jenny! Wow, Jenny. You're here.

BARBARA. *(nervous)* Can I get you a cup of coffee, Jenny? We are so surprised to see you! Jack just got up. A glass of water? It's so lovely to see you! It really is.

JENNY. Thanks for calling, Lorna. I was really worried about where Jack was. I've been trying to get a hold of him for days but he's not answering his cell. So it was terrific, you know, just great to find out he was here. With you. I thought, of course, why didn't I figure that out immediately, that he would come running home to his mommy in Cincinnati.

(This is met with a disappointed silence.)

LORNA. Wow.

BARBARA. Well. I guess you two need to talk. If you need anything –

JACK. Hang on, hang on.

(then)

Can I tell you something, Jenny? That was rude. What you just said? To my mom? That was, we don't talk like that, here.

JENNY. Oh, really.

JACK. Yeah, really. There are no lawyers here, making it okay for everybody to be shitty. And we're not in your family's home, we're in my family's home. People act different here. And you know what? You weren't invited.

JENNY. I am not playing games with you, Jack.

JACK. This is my mom's house. She never complained, okay she complained a little, but not without reason, because you've always been really rude to her, and it hurt her feelings. We're not doing that anymore.

BARBARA. Jack –

JACK. I didn't invite her, Mom!

JENNY. Your sister –

JACK. My sister accidentally mentioned to you where I was when she called you to tell you that she was sorry to hear that we were splitting up. That's not an invitation. That's good manners, something you might take note of, someday. You don't have any rights here. So, you be nice to my mom, and my sister, or I'm going to ask you to leave.

(There is a pause.)

JENNY. Did you tell them what you did?

(beat)

JACK. You are divorcing me. You have taken the position that you don't want to be a part of me, or this family, any more. So you don't get to ask questions about what we talk about.

JENNY. He stole twenty-seven million dollars.

(beat)

JACK. I didn't steal anything.

JENNY. You stole twenty-seven million dollars. So don't you lecture me about manners.

(another beat)

BARBARA. Jack?

JACK. I didn't.

JENNY. He stole twenty-seven million dollars.

LORNA. Jack?

(beat)

Jack?

JACK. Lorna. Lorna. Listen to me. Remember what I said.

(beat)

The truth is complicated.

(Blackout.)

End of Act One

ACT TWO

Scene One

(Things and people are where we left them. **BARBARA** *and* **LORNA** *are staring at* **JACK**.*)*

BARBARA. You stole?

JACK. Mom, it's not what it sounds like.

LORNA. What is it then?

JACK. It truly is so complicated, it's hardly worth explaining.

BARBARA. I don't believe it.

JACK. And you shouldn't because she is putting a completely negative spin on it.

JENNY. Oh, please.

LORNA. You stole –

JACK. That's not what happened!

JENNY. It is exactly what happened!

BARBARA. You stole.

JENNY. Yes.

JACK. No.

BARBARA. You stole.

JENNY. Yes.

JACK. No!

BARBARA. Oh, Jack.

(She sits.)

JACK. Mom. No no no. Mom, it's not as bad as she says.

LORNA. Not as bad as she says! Did you do it?

JACK. No!

JENNY. You told me about it yourself, you asshole! You confessed!

JACK. I told you what happened, that's not the same as "confessing." Besides, they're not pressing charges.

JENNY. It's not up to them, Jack! It's up to the attorney general's office! And they tend to take grand larceny seriously!

JACK. *(dismissing this)* Grand larceny.

JENNY. Grand larceny, yes, GRAND LARCENY.

BARBARA. Twenty-seven. Million?

JACK. There is an exact figure involved, yes – but –

JENNY. And that exact figure is twenty-seven million dollars.

LORNA. So what did you, what, did you embezzle it?

JENNY. Yes.

JACK. No. Not technically, no. There are similarities.

LORNA. What kind of similarities?

JACK. They're hard to explain to a lay person.

LORNA. Maybe you should try anyway, Jack! Just tell us what happened, would you, just tell us!

JACK. It's dead accounts.

> *(beat)*

They're all just – dead accounts.

> *(He shrugs, gets himself a beer out of the refrigerator.)*

BARBARA. Is that the explanation?

LORNA. YES IS THAT THE EXPLANATION?

JACK. Okay.

Okay! This is how it works. People die. And then there's a funeral.

LORNA. Jack, I swear –

JACK. You want me to do this just let me do this –

LORNA. *(overlap)* I want you to do it and not take forever and torture us –

JACK. *(overlap)* People die or forget or paperwork gets lost, who knows, no one knows, there's an explanation out there, no one cares, in every bank you end up with dead accounts, accounts that have no movement or action on them for you know a long time, the person attached to the account is just not there anymore. So, it's nobody's money.

JENNY. It's the bank's money.

JACK. It's not the bank's money.

JENNY. *(snapping)* It is clearly the bank's money, the money has been entrusted to the bank, it is legally owned as an asset by the bank –

JACK. Okay we're not going to get into the nuances. Let's just say it serves the bank to consider this money in these dead accounts its own money.

JENNY. Because it IS the bank's money. You stole money from a bank. You're a bank robber.

BARBARA. Oh, Jack.

JACK. Mom, trust me, it's not as bad as she's pretending!

JENNY. I'm not pretending!

JACK. Would you stop it? You're scaring my mom.

JENNY. She should be scared.

BARBARA. Well, I am. I really am. And you're not helping. None of this. This is a terrible time for us. Your father is in trouble! And this is why you don't want to see him, isn't it, why you wouldn't even go up and say hello! Because you're ashamed.

JACK. I'm not ashamed, actually.

BARBARA. Well, you should be.

JACK. Mom.

BARBARA. Explain to your sister. I don't have time. I have to go check on your father.

(She goes.)

JACK. *(to LORNA)* Maybe you should go up there with her.

LORNA. You go with her.

JACK. You go with her.

LORNA. I'm not doing it. You do it.

JACK. You do it.

LORNA. Make me.

JENNY. OKAY. Where were we? Robbing banks?

JACK. See, that's what I mean. That's so desperado, which is not accurate in this situation.

LORNA. Look, if you're just going to keep saying nothing then you might as well get up there and face Dad because you're going to have to tell him about this sooner or later –

JACK. OKAY. I'm doing it, I'm telling it.

(He sighs.)

Say you don't have anything to do one day, and you, you know, are trolling through account files – and let's just say you start to think about all that money in all those dead accounts and how it doesn't belong to anyone –

(cutting JENNY off before she can blurt)

– any PERSON in particular and the other thing you should know about dead accounts is nobody is really tracking them. People, the bank, it's just something that's there, that no one is paying any attention to. None of them. And who are "they," anyway? There is not even any "they," just an amorphous they, a they that floats. The people who own the money don't exist, and the people who make the money grow don't exist or at least they don't ever touch the money, there is like this completely ambiguous space between them and the money. But the money, even while it's floating around does exist. It can land. It can attain reality. If you detach it from death, or space, or no one. If you moved the money to another account. A little bit at a time. Maybe that would go unnoticed. And maybe you just do that once, to see? And when it does go unnoticed, you try it again. And then it's like that.

LORNA. *(appalled)* Until you get up to twenty-seven million?

JENNY. Until you get caught.

JACK. More like, until you get fired.

JENNY. How about, until you get sent to jail?

LORNA. Oh my God, Jack. You did. You embezzled money.

JACK. Okay, this is where your lack of technical information is limiting your understanding.

LORNA. I don't have a limited understanding, I get it! You stole a bunch of money from people who don't care about it.

JACK. Yes. Yes! That is –

LORNA. It's illegal is what it is! It's totally illegal, and you're going to jail!

JACK. See you think things like that, people in the middle of the country think things like that. But that's not how it works. This is why they think we're stupid. You think they think we're stupid because of things like, we believe in God, and we use mayonnaise in our cooking. But that's not really why. They think we're stupid because we still think you have to go to jail for stealing. What they know is that you can steal, and get caught, and not go to jail, AND get to keep the money. That's what they know, that we don't know, and they think we're stupid for not knowing it.

JENNY. You are going to jail. And you're not keeping that money.

JACK. Yet another thing you and I will have to agree to disagree about, my love.

(BARBARA enters. She looks at them.)

LORNA. Mom! How's he doing?

JACK. Seriously, Mom, I know you have a thing about it, I know you don't like it, but he's passing a kidney stone. You have to give him the pain killers.

BARBARA. I don't think that's going to do any good. He's not breathing.

BARBARA. *(cont.)*

(beat)

He's not breathing. HE'S NOT BREATHING.

(A beat as they take this in.)

(Blackout.)

Scene Two

(The kitchen, six hours later. JENNY is alone, on the telephone.)

JENNY. That's what he said! Can you believe that? "The truth is complicated." I'm thinking, not so complicated that they can't send you to jail, you jerk. Yes, I rea – I know, Stuart, but after everything I did for him, my family? My father! My father got him that job. Oh do not tell him I'm here, he will have an aneurysm if he – yes, I know, but of course I feel, I'm not – no, Jack's not here. I mean, he is here, I saw him, but he's not here right now. I walked in the front door, and before I could say three words there was this very convenient story about his father, and a kidney stone, and they all rushed off to some hospital. I mean, he did seem to be in some pain so what do I know, but I thought it was pretty coincidental, and I would not put it past Jack to actually give his father a kidney stone just to avoid dealing with this. He walked off with twenty-seven million dollars from a major international financial institution, and nobody apparently can figure out how he did it. I think a kidney stone is relatively simple next to that. I know – I KNOW I sound ridiculous but I'm truly at my wit's end, Stuart. I've been sitting here for eight hours, by myself, in this house, why do people live in houses like this in the Midwest, you should see this place. There actually is, seriously, linoleum floors. Linoleum, it's not a myth. And the cabinets are horrible.

(She presses a button on the wall. The garbage disposal roars. She jumps, backs away. BARBARA enters. She doesn't see her.)

(laughing)

Sorry, sorry, I have no idea what that was. But get this: There are little ceramic plates on the walls with pictures painted on them, I'm not making this up. And the flatware is just, I don't understand it. I don't know what it's made of. Some sort of strange gray metal. Oh, oh, and the dishes are Corelle. It says on the back of them: Corelle. I don't know what "Corelle" is, that's my point! It's just so deliberately without taste.

And yes there are yards with grass and trees, Jack used to go on endlessly about all the grass and trees and air in the Midwest but honestly I always found him to be needlessly smug about that stuff. Nature, like they invented nature. When they didn't invent it at all; let's face it, it's just here. Big deal. A fucking tree. Big fucking –

LORNA. *(entering)* Mom, seriously, the garage door needs new batteries. Jack's here; he can do it. Or apparently he can pay to have it done, I don't care how it happens but –

(**JENNY** *turns at the sound of her voice. She sees* **BARBARA**. **LORNA** *enters behind her.)*

JENNY. *(on phone)* Stuart, I'm going to have to go. I'll call you back.

(beat)

Me too.

(She hangs up.)

BARBARA. *(pointing)* Those are the kitchen dishes. I have a lovely set, bone china, from Germany with gold leaf. I keep it in the dining room, in the china cabinet. We got it for our wedding, forty seven years ago, and I haven't lost even one dish. And the "flatware" is made of stainless steel. I don't know what that is, actually, but it's hardly a new invention. And just for the record I have a very nice set of silverware. Which is silver! That stays in the dining room too.

LORNA. What happened?

BARBARA. She doesn't like trees. I'm going to go pack a suitcase for your father.

(But **BARBARA** *is gone.* **LORNA** *looks back to* **JENNY**.*)*

LORNA. You don't like trees?

(She takes off her coat and drapes it on a chair.)

JENNY. I was just using the phone. My cell can't seem to pick up a signal here. Ohio! You'd think because it was so flat and the buildings are so short – never mind. How, how is your father?

LORNA. They did a lot of tests and admitted him. God I could use a drink. I think we have some wine around here somewhere. You want some?

(She goes to the refrigerator, gets some wine out.)

JENNY. Oh. I. No, thank you.

LORNA. I hate hospitals. Everything is so clean and dire. I went out for a Diet Mountain Dew at one point and came back and all these people rushed up to me, said "who are you who are you" and I was like, my father is over there, passing a kidney stone. And so they go Oh! Okay, great. Carry on. Turns out in the room right here, right next to him, someone had just died. Seriously I looked over and there was a dead body and people washing their hands.

(She starts to laugh.)

JENNY. That's horrible.

LORNA. Oh, what a day.

JENNY. But he's all right?

LORNA. They pumped him full of morphine and shot sound waves at him. Wonder how much that's gonna cost.

(a beat, sober)

Jack stole twenty-seven million dollars. He really did, didn't he?

JENNY. Yes. He did.

*(***LORNA*** *starts to laugh again.)*

I'm calling the police. Now. I'm calling them right now.

(She starts to dial.)

LORNA. Wait, wait, sorry. Why?

JENNY. Why? Because he's a thief and he's on the run and that's the sort of thing that is frowned on, actually, in legal circles.

LORNA. He's not on the run. Would you relax? Put that down. Jesus, my father's in the hospital on a ventilator.

Do you think you could have a heart and not call the police right this very second. Thank you.

(She takes the phone from **JENNY** *and puts it on the counter.)*

JENNY. He's on a ventilator?

LORNA. Actually no, he's sleeping peacefully. But seriously, I do not want to talk to the cops right now. I think it would be bad, if they showed up. I think it would upset people.

JENNY. Well, where is Jack?

LORNA. He went out for pizza.

JENNY. Well, excuse me, but I don't particularly feel like taking that statement at face value.

LORNA. Okay, fine.

(handing her the phone)

If you want to call the cops, go ahead. You know, frankly, I don't know why you haven't done it, already. Why didn't you call the cops in New York, when you found out what he did?

JENNY. I wanted to give him a chance.

LORNA. A chance for what?

JENNY. A chance to redeem himself.

LORNA. You know, if my mom said that to me, I would know what it meant, but I actually don't know what it means, when you say it.

JENNY. Trust me. Jack will know.

LORNA. Yeah, okay.

(*beat*)

So what's the problem with trees?

JENNY. That is not what I said.

LORNA. I mean, I don't know why you would not like trees.

JENNY. I do like trees.

LORNA. That one over there, the maple? I planted that tree. Jack planted this one, right here. It's a sycamore.

JENNY. Really.

LORNA. Yes, really, we got these sticks at school, on Arbor Day, they gave everybody these sticks and you brought them home and planted them. Boy, that was a long time ago. It was such a cold day. You know that sort of terrible wet spring chill that we used to get before global warming? Maybe it wasn't that cold, maybe we just didn't have good coats. But that's what I remember, shivering out there. And the dirt, under your nails, patting the ground around that poor little stick, and Dad saying, one day a long time from now, this stick will be a tree. I asked him how long, like a year? And he laughed and said, more like twenty-five years. It sounded insane to me, honestly. Plant this poor little stick in the ground and in twenty-five years you will have a tree? Madness. Besides, when you're six years old, you think twenty-five years is like death, you know. I mean you don't think you'll be dead. But you think somehow you'll be gone. Even if that stick actually does become a tree, you won't see it. But there it is. My tree. Jack's tree. Dad was right.

(*then*)

You ever plant a tree?

JENNY. (*a sigh*) No, I never did. You ever take violin lessons?

LORNA. What's that got to do with anything?

JENNY. Just a question.

LORNA. Why did you ask that question?

JENNY. No reason.

LORNA. You had a reason. It sounded like you wanted to make a point, like you never planted a tree but I never took violin lessons. When, what do they have to do with each other?

JENNY. I wasn't trying to make a point.

LORNA. I've been in the hospital all day! My father is really sick! Something is wrong! His system is, it's failing him, he is failing! And he's in pain, he's suffering! He's not even a person anymore, he's just pain! My mother is frightened! Death is coming here. You and your stupid dead accounts. We got the real thing coming here. And it's my dad, my good dad, my...

(She has to stop herself, or she'll start crying.)

JENNY. Okay, Okay!

LORNA. It's not okay. It's not.

(then)

So was that your boyfriend? On the phone?

JENNY. What?

LORNA. The person you were saying all those things to.

JENNY. That was my lawyer.

LORNA. You said "me too." At the end of the phone call. Like he said, "I love you," and you said back to him, "me too."

JENNY. People say 'me too' on the phone, Lorna.

LORNA. I don't.

(PHIL appears in the door, carrying eight boxes of pizza. The pile of boxes obscures his face.)

Oh, for crying out loud, Jack. I told you. One pizza. ONE PIZZA.

PHIL. Not Jack. It's me, Phil.

LORNA. Phil?

(PHIL sets down the boxes.)

PHIL. Yeah, Jack picked me up on his way to La Rosa's.

LORNA. Well, why did you let him buy all this?

PHIL. Well, he doesn't actually do what I tell him.

(JACK *enters behind him, carrying grocery bags.*)

JACK. No one ever agrees! There has to be one pepperoni and one sausage, and one vegetarian, just to start. But actually you need two pepperoni, because that's the one that everyone likes so that evaporates even if you buy two. Mom likes that crazy chicken pizza, which she managed to mention fifteen times at the hospital and she never gets to have it because Dad doesn't like it. Jenny likes fresh garlic, which you hate. It's La Rosa's, so you have to get one Sicilian. So what are we up to, six? Seven? It was like that.

LORNA. Jack, this is stupid!

JACK. It's not as stupid as you're making it sound.

LORNA. Yes it is. First of all, there aren't seven thousand brothers and sisters here anymore so the pepperoni pizza is NOT going to evaporate, and Sharon's not here either insisting on a vegetarian pizza that no one is going to eat. Jenny IS here but she doesn't eat at all, no one has ever seen her eat anything and I don't believe that even if there is garlic on a pizza she will eat it. And Mom DOES like the chicken pizza but I like it too, so you were supposed to get ONE chicken pizza. ONE CHICKEN PIZZA.

(*She is really angry.* JACK *looks at her, puts his arm around her.*)

JACK. (*reasonable, even kind*) We can freeze it, then Mom doesn't have to cook. She's got her hands full and she doesn't need to think about cooking right now. And frankly, it's reassuring, when things suck, to have comfort food around the house.

LORNA. Yeah but it makes the house crowded. Now the kitchen is crowded, it's crowded with pizza. I feel like I'm suffocating.

JACK. That's not the pizza, that's my glowering wife. Hi sweetheart. You want a slice of pizza?

(He kisses her on the cheek, quick.)

JENNY. No. Thank you.

LORNA. See?

PHIL. I'd love a slice. Hi, I'm Phil.

(He shakes **JENNY**'s *hand.)*

LORNA. You want a plate?

PHIL. Not if it's any trouble.

LORNA. A plate? How can a plate be trouble?

(She goes to the cabinet. Behind her back **JACK** *gives* **PHIL** *the thumbs up sign.)*

JENNY. Jack, we need to talk.

JACK. Oh, now she wants to talk. I've been trying to talk to her for two years. Didn't realize quite what it would take to get her attention.

JENNY. This is a very bad situation that you've put yourself in. And me too, you've put me in a terrible situation. And I appreciate that you are having some sort of family – crisis – here, that is unfortunate, but Lorna tells me that your father is going to be fine, for now, so you and I need to go back to New York and deal with this.

PHIL. Can I get a beer or something?

LORNA. There's a box of wine in the refrigerator.

PHIL. Oh, that would be great.

(She goes for the glasses.)

JENNY. Jack, are you even listening to me?

JACK. I am listening but I'm not going back to New York with you, so you need to get that idea out of your head. I fucking hate New York and I'm not going back.

JENNY. That is not up to you! You committed a crime, you can't just flee the jurisdiction! If they find out, you won't even get bail!

PHIL. Jack – committed a crime?

LORNA. He stole twenty-seven million dollars.

PHIL. Really?

JENNY. Yes, really. He stole it from the bank. He's a bank robber.

LORNA. You know, you actually do have to stop acting like that's such a terrible thing, Jenny. No one in the Midwest gives a shit about banks right now. They've been behaving very badly and they act like it doesn't matter that people's lives are being ruined because all they cared about was their profits and bonuses and taking all the bailout money and now no one can get a loan because they don't give a shit about people, so we don't give a shit about them. So don't go acting like it's so terrible he stole from a bank. No one here cares.

JACK. Thank you!

LORNA. I'm not on your side either. You stole money, you jerk. And I don't care if you do think I'm stupid for thinking this, but that usually does mean going to jail.

JACK. Only in the Midwest.

LORNA. Well, that's where you are right now. I hope you have a good lawyer.

JACK. I have a lot of lawyers. I have about six divorce lawyers.

JENNY. Okay. This is not about the divorce.

JACK. Are you sure?

JENNY. I did not fly all the way to Cincinnati to talk to you about our divorce.

JACK. Because some clever therapist might observe that I started siphoning funds right about when my wife declared that she was walking away from our marriage.

JENNY. Jack!

JACK. Or the fact that maybe I started grabbing all that money because I needed something to put in my heart to make up for the fact that you stomped all over it!

(BARBARA enters.)

BARBARA. Has anyone called Sharon, or Karen, or Doug, or Beth?

(She goes to the refrigerator.)

LORNA. I talked to Beth at the hospital. She was going to call Sharon and Sharon can call Karen and Doug. What are you doing?

BARBARA. I'm making up a bag, for your father. I wanted to bring him something to eat, the food in those hospitals is always so terrible.

LORNA. He's sleeping, Mom, you can leave it until the morning.

BARBARA. When he wakes up he's going to be hungry.

LORNA. That's hours from now; would you relax? You're the one who should eat something. Here, we got the chicken pizza you like.

(She finds it for her and makes her a plate.)

BARBARA. Look at all this! Why did you buy so much?

LORNA. I didn't do it. Jack did it, remember. Jack went for the pizza.

JACK. It's comfort food.

BARBARA. I don't even know what that means. What are we going to do with all this pizza?

JACK. You freeze it, pizza freezes, and then you'll have it, so you won't have to cook.

BARBARA. Your father doesn't eat pizza.

JACK. Not for him, then, for you.

BARBARA. I eat what he eats! What are we going to do with all this?

JACK. Don't worry about it, Mom.

BARBARA. How can I not worry about it? It's everywhere. And now it's just going to go to waste. Jack you just waste everything. Waste. Waste!

(There is a sad silence.)

PHIL. *(stepping up)* I'll take it home with me. It would be great to have some food in the freezer. Cause you know. You really don't feel like cooking at the end of a long work day. And I actually really love pizza. Jack's right, I find it totally comforting.

BARBARA. *(looking at him)* Oh, Phil. I'm sorry. I didn't know you were here.

PHIL. Hi, Mrs. Leonard.

BARBARA. How are you dear, we haven't seen you in a while.

PHIL. I've been busy.

BARBARA. Are you still at P and G?

PHIL. Yes.

BARBARA. They're so good to their employees.

PHIL. Yes they are.

BARBARA. What do you do for them, dear?

PHIL. Well, I'm, actually, I'm an accountant.

BARBARA. Oh, an accountant! So you work accounts?

PHIL. That pretty much covers it.

BARBARA. Jack does that too.

PHIL. So I've heard.

BARBARA. Not quite as successfully as you, apparently.

JACK. Or more so.

BARBARA. Maybe you could help him out.

PHIL. I think what he's talking about is a little beyond me.

BARBARA. Then you've heard about all of this.

PHIL. Some of it. Not all of it. I was sorry to hear about Mr. Leonard being so sick.

BARBARA. It's really been difficult.

PHIL. I'm sure it has. Here, you sit down and have some food, and let me get all these boxes out of the way. I'm just going to put them in the dining room, all right?

BARBARA. Thank you, sweetheart.

PHIL. *(to LORNA)* Maybe your mom would like a little glass of that wine.

LORNA. *(stunned)* Sure.

(He starts to stack up the pizza while she gets the wine.)

PHIL. I'm just going to leave the chicken pizza right here since I hear that's the one you like.

(He takes some of the others and goes.)

JENNY. Barbara, look. I cannot tell you how sorry I am to be bringing more trouble into your house when you're dealing with this illness, but what Jack has done is quite serious.

BARBARA. You don't have to tell me that. I've been upstairs praying about it.

JENNY. Oh. Good.

BARBARA. Jack committed a crime.

JACK. That's strong, Mom. It is true that the bank is not happy about certain things, but about a lot of it, I'm pretty much innocent.

JENNY. You are not!

JACK. It's only stealing if you accept that taking that money out of those accounts was stealing. Which is not necessarily the way everyone will see it.

BARBARA. You took money that wasn't yours.

JACK. I took money that wasn't anybody's.

BARBARA. Money belongs to someone.

JACK. You think that, but that's not necessarily true.

BARBARA. You listen to me, young man. What you did was a sin. You have to give that money away.

JACK. Give it away to who?

BARBARA. To the poor.

JACK. The poor? Why should they get it?

BARBARA. You made a mistake, honey. Maybe you didn't mean to.

LORNA. How could he not mean to?

BARBARA. But you could make it up. And free your heart.

(PHIL *slips back in the room.*)

LORNA. He has to give the money back to the bank, Mom.

(*to* JENNY)

That will fix things, right. If he just gives the money back?

JENNY. I don't... know. There's a lot we have to work out.

BARBARA. We, what do you mean, we?

JENNY. Well – my family has a lot of relationships, my father actually was the one who got Jack the job, frankly, at that bank, and he knows a lot of people at that bank.

BARBARA. He must be furious with him! You're getting a divorce and now Jack's stolen all this money, your father isn't going to help Jack.

JENNY. Nevertheless Jack does need to come back to New York so that we can untangle this situation the best way possible.

BARBARA. Why? Why can't he just stay here, with his own family, we're the ones who can help him. And you can do all that banking on the telephone, or over wires or something. That's what we did here, when we refinanced the house. The money came from New York but we didn't have to go there. Jack, where is all this money?

JACK. You know, Mom, I can't actually say. Because what Jenny isn't telling you is that she doesn't want me to give the money back. As part of the divorce settlement, she thinks she has a right to it. And I haven't told her where it is, so she can't find it! And that's really what she's mad about. Not about the law, or the bank. She knows the bank doesn't really care about the money, to the bank, twenty-seven million dollars is not actually very much money! So, she doesn't want me to give it back to them. She wants me to give it to her.

(beat)

BARBARA. I think I need to pray some more.

JACK. Okay, but if God tells you anything about me going to jail, he's lying.

JENNY. You will be going to jail if you don't do the right thing, right now.

JACK. I'm not going to jail, and I am not giving you one red cent.

BARBARA. I'm not sure I understand.

JACK. Go pray about it, Mom.

BARBARA. I really do think you should give it to the poor.

(She goes. JACK looks at JENNY.)

JENNY. I'm done playing with you. You tell me where that money is or I will fuck up your life so bad you'll wish you were never born. You will curse the day you ever laid eyes on me.

JACK. I already do.

JENNY. Where is that fucking money?

(PHIL and LORNA glance at each other.)

LORNA. Phil, can I show you the yard?

PHIL. I'd love that. I love your yard.

(They exit out the back door. JACK looks at JENNY.)

JENNY. I'm calling the cops right now. I'm serious.

JACK. You're not calling the cops on me.

JENNY. Jack, you cannot continue to maintain the position, that you have a right to keep all that money that you stole!

JACK. I do maintain that. I stole it; it's mine.

JENNY. Okay. Fine. Okay. Then you give me no motivation whatsoever to protect you from legal action.

JACK. Protect me! That's a laugh. For the last two years you've been doing everything you could to take me down.

JENNY. I am not going to get dragged into some recriminatory file cabinet about who did what to who, Jack.

JACK. *(laughing)* No no no, got to stay out of the file cabinet. That's the only thing either of us ever learned from that fucking couples counselor: Anytime anyone has anything to say, it's off limits because of that that fucking file cabinet. Well, fuck that we're on my turf now and I have a few things to say about our marriage.

JENNY. Yes I am aware –

JACK. *(in the clear)* YOU ARE MY WIFE. I AM YOUR HUSBAND. And I don't mean that, you know, God you look at me like that is some terrible thing to say but we were married, we chose each other, we are part of each other, in an equation, two parts of a whole, that is what we promised to be to each other in whatever crazy ceremony that was –

JENNY. It was a highly respected humanistic ceremony! The ethical culture society! We talked about it, Jack. This is why it's pointless to get into the file cabinet, because you can drown there, we talked about the ceremony and we both agreed that we were happy with the ethical culture society because they were serious and they wouldn't say the word God.

JACK. Yes, I remember that was important to you.

JENNY. It was important to both of us! You didn't want a Catholic wedding, you had a lot of issues!

JACK. A lot of people have issues with the Catholic Church I'm hardly alone in that but that doesn't mean that God is off the table.

JENNY. This is so not the point. Going back to the beginning, to the file cabinet –

JACK. It seemed holy, I didn't want God to be left out of it, I wanted to stand before God and declare you were the partner of my life! Why can't we talk about that?

JENNY. Because we're getting a divorce.

JACK. I'm AWARE. And that means I'm not allowed to talk about God, I'm not allowed to talk about who we are together –

JENNY. Jack, we were happy, and then we stopped being happy, and that is no one's fault, it is just what happened, it had nothing to do with anything like like like

JACK. Like what? Like your fucking family hated me on sight?

JENNY. Oh, sort of like your family did?

JACK. My family is NICE. They may have hated you but they would have loved you in spite of hating you. We're in the Midwest,we're too polite to be mean. That's less of a problem on the east coast.

JENNY. My family welcomed you.

JACK. "Welcome" is a barbecue in the backyard. It is not a dinner at twenty-one. Where everyone wants to know where you went to college and what 'house' you were in.

JENNY. This is meaningless. This is why we don't go into the file cabinet. I know, I am well aware, that there were aspects of your transition to New York which were a little rocky for you. That is not, frankly, what I am here to talk to you about.

JACK. I loved you.

JENNY. JACK!

JACK. Oh, that's not, now it's not even okay to admit that we fell in love, that our marriage began, it began in love –

JENNY. *(overriding)* I just don't think it's useful, Jack!

JACK. Is that why you tell a person you love them? Because it's useful? "Oh, here's a useful thing, I'll tell Jenny I love her; that will get me what I want."

JENNY. *(furious)* No it won't!

JACK. Why couldn't we move to Brooklyn.

JENNY. Oh for crying out loud.

JACK. *(overlap)* I wasn't saying let's move to Ohio; I wasn't saying let's move back to Cincinnati –

JENNY. Yes, because I would have laughed at you!

JACK. *(overlap)* But what's wrong with Brooklyn? Those brownstones are elegant.

JENNY. Jack, you didn't grow up on Manhattan so you never understood. But it's Brooklyn.

JACK. You could have a whole house, and a, not a yard, but a garden. We could have had kids there.

JENNY. What are you doing? Why are you going over this? It's done. We're done. You know we're done. And I want my money.

JACK. It's not your money.

JENNY. Half of what's yours is mine.

JACK. *(furious)* Half of my HEART? ONLY HALF?

JENNY. Okay. Okay. I'm sorry we don't understand each other anymore. I, we did love each other, at the beginning, I want you to know that, I really had strong feelings for you. You swept me off my feet. And perhaps I was naive about how different we were. But you know, so were you. And by the way, you can complain now, about my family, and all the money, but you liked it. When we – you were happy to get out of the Midwest. You were desperate for New York. And you were happy there.

JACK. *(quiet)* I was happy.

JENNY. So that changed for you. You never told me why.

(beat)

JACK. It wasn't – big enough. All the red meat, the food, the money, the concrete, staring at a computer screen all day and getting drunk every night with people you don't like, and the constant, it was so – demeaning, the way people talked to each other, so much noise, everyone sweating all day in those expensive suits, and typing and laughing at things that weren't funny, nobody could tell a fucking joke, my head felt, all the time, a kind of something behind my eyes like a disease or an insect burrowing... And not just behind my eyes, in my bloodstream, a kind of toxic- millions of dollars meaning nothing because we never saw it or held it or used it for anything but pleasure that we couldn't even feel anymore because nothing, the fury attached to nothing, I felt it all going there, it was the only place there for any of it to go, to where we are nothing and the money is the only thing – and we are just reptiles. Carrion birds. Screaming. Around it. It's stupid. To live your life like that? Isn't it? No boundaries. Just hunger. It's stupid.

JENNY. What's stupid is breaking the law.

JACK. *(nodding)* Unless you get away with it.

JENNY. But you didn't.

JACK. Didn't I?

JENNY. No.

JACK. And yet, I know where all that money is, and nobody else does.

JENNY. They are going to find it, Jack!

JACK. They haven't yet.

JENNY. My father will protect you!

JACK. No he won't.

JENNY. Yes he will but you have to work with us.

JACK. You mean I have to give you half the money.

JENNY. The percentage is negotiable.

JACK. Meaning he wants MORE than half.

JENNY. Do you want to walk away from this or not?

JACK. I already did, Jenny! For two years I sat in that cubicle and siphoned off money, and nobody noticed, and nobody cared, they kept paying me for fuck's sake!

JENNY. Unless you have someone fix this for you, you will go to jail.

JACK. Fix it for a price.

JENNY. Fix it!

JACK. Tell you what. Your dad sent you here to negotiate with me, I get it. Tell him this for me: I'll give you half the money, when you give me half that fucking teapot.

JENNY. I don't know what you are talking about.

JACK. The Mayflower teapot, yet another thing that disappeared from the bank. I want half of it. And I mean half. I want him to take an acetylene torch, and cut that fucking teapot in half, and when he gives me my half of his teapot, I will give him your half of the money I stole.

JENNY. I am not going to tell him that.

JACK. Okay, then you know what I want? I want you. Half of you. No wait no wait. All of you, for one minute. One kiss, for one minute.

JENNY. Oh for fuck's sake!

JACK. The way you used to kiss me. That's what I want. Like a fairy tale. I want one kiss. Like a frog. You give me a kiss, I'll give you the gold.

JENNY. Jack –

JACK. What, are you going to argue with that? Because it's a great deal, a fucking awesome offer. One kiss. But it has to be a real one. You know, not a fake little peck, we're not going to mess around here.

JENNY. Yes, I understand that that is not your style.

JACK. You want to, come on. I want a kiss, now. Come on.

JENNY. Don't push me! You always push.

JACK. I push because I'm right.

JENNY. You push because you're pushy.

JACK. You –

JENNY. Jack do you think that for just one minute you could just shut up?

(He shuts up and waits, while she considers this. The wait is a shred too excruciating. Finally, she approaches him. They consider each other. She leans in carefully and kisses him with some caution. At which point he catches her around the waist. They look at each other. He kisses her. After a moment, it grows.)

(They continue to kiss, which becomes spectacularly intimate and passionate. They end up on the kitchen table, absolutely making out. They stop, finally, exhausted.)

I can't do this.

JACK. *(tender)* Stay with me, Jenny.

JENNY. I am not – living in Cincinnati.

(She pulls away from him.)

JACK. It doesn't have to be Cincinnati. It could be anywhere. Anywhere in the world. As long as we're together. Just stay with me.

JENNY. *(simple)* You have to give me the money, Jack. You just do. My father didn't send me. He doesn't know I'm here! But you know him he won't stop. He will, he will just keep coming after you.

JACK. So you are protecting me.

JENNY. Just give me the money. Give me half of it. I can get him to back down, if you'll just give me half. You'll still have millions!

JACK. I'm not giving you the money.

JENNY. *(mad)* I kissed you!

JACK. You kissed me because you wanted to, because you love me. I'm not paying for that kiss.

JENNY. Well, that's just – great.

(JENNY *stands up, thinks about saying something mean. She shakes her head then, and starts to look for her purse. He grabs her.*)

JACK. Jenny. Listen to me. I'm telling you the truth now. You didn't come here to get the money. You came for me. It doesn't matter that you're from New York and I'm from the Midwest. Love can transcend that.

JENNY. It can't.

JACK. It can! Stay with me. Be with me. That money is ours, It's for both of us. I stole it for us. We can be together with that money, we can be anywhere. We can protect each other.

JENNY. I'm sorry. I can't do that. I just can't.

(*And with that, she picks up her purse, and goes.*)

JACK. Don't leave. Come on. Jenny. Don't leave!

(*But she is gone. He goes after her. After a moment,* **LORNA** *and* **PHIL** *enter from the backyard, cautious.*)

LORNA. Is the coast clear?

PHIL Yes.

LORNA. Thank God.

PHIL. They still love each other.

LORNA. I know. It's too bad.

PHIL. You okay?

LORNA. It's not usually like this, here. Usually it's just a lot quieter.

PHIL. I would hope so.

LORNA. No, no. There's actually something kind of thrilling about it. Because honestly, Mom and Dad don't have a lot going on. I drive Mom to the grocery store, or the library. Sometimes I go to the pharmacy and pick up a prescription. It's hideous, truth be told. It's positively horrible.

(She starts to cry just the littlest bit.)

PHIL. Oh, no –

LORNA. *(getting it together)* I mean, I don't, of course you can't approve of what Jack did. Stealing? I don't care what he says about 'Oh in New York no one cares about that.' It is breaking the law.

PHIL. Exactly.

LORNA. But on the other hand, at least things happen, when he's around. Nothing happens to me here. I'm like a servant here. Seriously! Plus my mother is insane. You must have noticed.

PHIL. No.

LORNA. Oh don't be polite. She's completely bananas.

PHIL. I think she's nice.

LORNA. She's nuts. And I'm going to be just like her. You think I don't know that? Oh God. I am, I'm turning out just like her.

PHIL. Well, I think she's nice, so I don't think that would be so terrible.

LORNA. Oh come on. She's bonkers. She's obsessed with God.

PHIL. So is half of America. Have you watched the news lately?

LORNA. I hate religion. It's the same thing as money. You know? It's just, the exact same thing. Religion and money are just the dumb things we use to plug up the hole in our hearts because we're so afraid of dying. But guess what? We're all going to die anyway. All of us! We're all going to DIE ANYWAY.

PHIL. Religion and money are the same thing. Wow. I never thought of it that way. That – is pretty smart, actually.

LORNA. But not brilliant. That's what my mother says. I'm smart but not brilliant. And I work hard.

PHIL. I think you're brilliant.

LORNA. Smart is what you said.

PHIL. You're smart and brilliant. That thing you told me about planting that tree? That was incredible. I mean, it was so beautiful. And true. Jack told me that everything he says is true, but I'm not so sure about him. But you –

LORNA. No, he does, he always tells the truth. Most of the time you want to smack him for it.

PHIL. When you tell the truth I don't want to smack you.

LORNA. That's nice but you know what? I have to get out of here. I do. I have to GO.

PHIL. You mean, like, leave?

LORNA. Why not? I'm just getting old here.

PHIL. You're not old.

LORNA. I didn't say I was old, I said I was getting old. I seriously I have to do something before it's too late.

PHIL. You planted that tree.

LORNA. That was twenty-five years ago!

PHIL. Yeah but you know, there's this Chinese proverb that says you wasted your life unless you have a child, write a book, or plant a tree. So, you already did one of those things. And you're young! You still have time, to do the other two.

LORNA. Then why am I so unhappy?

PHIL. I don't think you are unhappy. I think you're bored. That doesn't mean you rob a bank.

It means you go to the movies once in a while. You look up an old friend and have some laughs. Come on, I'll take you to the movies. We'll have a good time. You'll feel better. I promise.

*(**LORNA** looks at him. Pause.)*

LORNA. Are you asking me out on a date?

*(**PHIL** thinks about this, then takes the plunge.)*

PHIL. Yes. I am asking you out on a date.

LORNA. Sure took you long enough.

PHIL. Well, I'm a full grown tree now.

(She laughs at this. He grins. After a moment, he moves over to her, leans in and kisses her. She laughs. They kiss again. It makes them both laugh.)

You know, I've – I've really liked you for a long time.

LORNA. *(smiling)* Me too.

*(**JACK** enters, silent. They look at him. He comes over, sits at the table. He is depressed.)*

*(A pause. **LORNA** goes to **JACK**, sits by him, puts her hand on his. **BARBARA** enters.)*

BARBARA. Did she go?

JACK. She didn't want to.

LORNA. Maybe – maybe you should just give them what they want, Jack. And be done with it.

JACK. No way. Seriously, they don't need the money. They're all so rich, they don't have anything to spend it on!

They have so much money they're exhausted by it. The money itself is exhausted. They just can't stand the fact that I beat them. I fucking beat them.

*(**JACK** stands, moves away, restless.)*

PHIL. You want a piece of pizza, Jack?

JACK. You know what I don't get? Why the things they tell you, when you're a kid, go away when you're an adult. Like, sharing. Kindness. Do your homework. Why do they teach you that stuff and then tell you you're stupid, when you're an adult, for believing any of it?

(He looks out the window.)

Boy, this yard is nice. That tree is so pretty.

LORNA. Give the money back!

JACK. Why should I?

LORNA. Because it's not YOURS. Everything that we learned, sharing and not cheating and doing your homework, and planting sticks on Arbor Day, that didn't go away. You abandoned it.

JACK. Arbor Day?

LORNA. Arbor Day. You can't even remember Arbor Day. Oh, forget it. You're one of them now, Jack. You're a fucking capitalist. And a thief. Phil, let's go.

PHIL. Where are we going?

LORNA. To the movies!

PHIL. Oh. Cool.

*(He glances back at **JACK**, can't think of anything to say, and follows her out the door. **JACK** sits there for a moment. **BARBARA** sighs, starts to clean the kitchen.)*

JACK. Okay Mom. Everybody else is taking shots. Let me have it.

BARBARA. Oh, honey. I'm not going to criticize. I'm your mother. I love you.

(then)

I don't know what your father's going to have to say about it.

JACK. Do we have to tell him?

BARBARA. Twenty-seven million dollars is a pretty big secret.

JACK. I'll give you two, just to keep your mouth shut.

(beat)

BARBARA. Oh. You're joking.

JACK. Am I? You can feed a lot of poor people for two million dollars, mom.

BARBARA. You kids.

(She continues to clean.)

You are going to have to talk to him, you know. You can't avoid it forever.

JACK. *(gentle)* I'm not afraid of talking to Dad, Mom. I'm really not. I just didn't want to bother him. He has a lot on his plate right now.

BARBARA. Yes he does.

(She chokes up, overwhelmed suddenly.)

JACK. Come on. Let me get you some ice cream.

BARBARA. I don't need any ice cream.

JACK. Everybody needs ice cream. It's one of the blessings of life. It really is. God's little benediction on a bad day.

BARBARA. *(a smile at this)* God?

JACK. You're so predictable, I knew that would get you on board. Vanilla, right? As I recall, you liked to keep things simple. Vanilla, for my mom.

BARBARA. I don't know.

JACK. I do.

(He goes to the freezer and finds the ice cream, gives it to her. She looks at it. Smiling, he sits next to her.)

And there's plenty more where that came from.

BARBARA. *(sudden)* There isn't more, Jack. Honey. There isn't more!

(They look at each other.)

JACK. You know those dead accounts? You know what I think? Those people escaped. They escaped the money. I just don't know how they did it.

BARBARA. Oh, Jack. Oh, my little boy. My good little boy.

(*She goes back into the house.* **JACK** *looks back at her, then at the ice cream.*)

JACK. The ice cream will help, Mom. You can have as much as you want. Mom. Mom! You can have anything. Anything? Wait a minute. Wait a minute. Arbor Day!

(*He looks upstage.*)

Right.

(**JACK** *sits at the table, broods. The walls of the kitchen shift, drift away. He is alone, at the table, under the branches of the giant tree.*)

(*Blackout.*)

End of Play